THE FIRE ENGINE BOOK

Pictures by
Tibor Gergely

A GOLDEN BOOK • NEW YORK
Golden Books Publishing Company, Inc., New York, New York 10106

Ding, ding, ding! goes the alarm.

The firemen slide down the pole.

Clang, clang, clang! goes the fire engine bell.

The chief is on his way.

Here they come!

Watch out! Make way for the hose car.

Hurry, hurry! Jump on the hook-and-ladder truck!

The people come running out to see

the great big hook-and-ladder truck.

Here they are at the fire.

The chief tells his men what to do.

Quick! Connect the hoses!

S-s-s-s! goes the water.

Crank, crank. Up go the ladders.

Up go the firemen with their hoses.

Chop, chop, chop! go the axes.

Crash! go the windows.

Down the ladders come the firemen.

They jump into the net to save things from the fire!

Sput, sput, sput! Out goes the fire.

Tired firemen and people go home.

Hurray for the brave firemen!